MULTICULTURAL READERS
SET 1

THE
TWIN

ANNE SCHRAFF

Artesian Press

P.O. Box 355 Buena Park, CA 90621

STANDING TALL MYSTERY SERIES
MULTICULTURAL READERS
SET 1

Project Editor: Carol E. Newell
Cover Illustrator: TSA Design Group
Cover Design: Tony Amaro
©2000 Artesian Press

 *Artesian Press*

ISBN 1-58659-081-2

Chapter 1

"Mariel!" Lauren Bailey cried, rushing up to Mariel Russell after first period. "Did you see the new girl?"

"What are you yelling about, girl?" Mariel asked with a laugh.

"It's amazing, Mariel! I mean it's like she's your twin sister! I just about dropped dead when I saw her. I almost yelled and said, 'Hey, Mariel, what are *you* doing in History first period? You're supposed to be in English!'"

"Who is this girl?" Mariel asked.

"Her name is Jannon Brown, and she's real mum about where she's from. But, Mariel, I swear, she's a dead ringer for you, honest!" Lauren said.

"This, I've got to see," Mariel said.

"There she is! She's right by the snack machine, and she's buying those little fig cookies—the ones you always go for. And she's wearing your color, too!"

"Hot pink, yeah," Mariel grumbled. "She's got her nerve wearing my color." Up to then it was a joke to Mariel, but when she drew closer to Jannon she gasped in astonishment. She was prepared for a girl who sort of resembled her, but Jannon could have been Mariel!

"Didn't I tell you? Didn't I tell you?" Lauren said. "It's weird, huh?"

Jannon turned and stared at Mariel. Finally, she said, "Hi."

"Hi," Mariel said slowly. She felt so strange. She was covered with goose bumps. She felt like she was looking in a mirror. Oh, there were small differences. Jannon was a tiny bit taller, more willowy. Maybe her cheekbones stood out a little more, but basically they were carbon copies of each other.

"I'm Jannon Brown," the girl said. "I'm new here at Grant ... uh ... we sorta look alike, don't we?"

Mariel shrugged. "I guess so."

"I hope you don't mind," Jannon said. "I mean everybody says you're really popular and stuff. Student officer, cheerleader ... everything."

"Mind? Why should I mind?" Mariel asked, the hair standing up on the back of her neck. Of course she minded! It is bad enough when somebody shows up at a party wearing the same kind of a dress you're wearing. But Jannon Brown had shown up at school wearing Mariel's face! It was like being caught in a science fiction nightmare, with Jannon as her clone!

Jannon came closer. She had big, brown velvety eyes—just like Mariel's. She had full lips, exactly like Mariel's. Mariel hated it—she couldn't believe this was happening to her. She read once that everybody has a look-alike somewhere in the world, but why did hers have to show up at her school?

"I hope we can be friends, Mariel," Jannon said.

"Yeah," Mariel muttered, glancing at her watch. "Oh, I'm late for Biology. I gotta run."

"I've got Biology this period, too," Jannon said.

"Oh, no," Mariel groaned to herself. This was the class Mariel's boyfriend, Terrell Mayfield, was in. He'd be staring at Jannon all through class, driving Mariel crazy. If only Jannon would sit in the front, next to that quiet boy, Ryan Brown. He didn't have a girlfriend. He and Jannon coincidentally had the same last name anyway. If only they'd strike up a friendship!

But Jannon plopped down in the last row, right beside Terrell Mayfield! Mariel's cheeks burned. It was as if Jannon was an evil clone who'd come here just to ruin Mariel's life, and all the while wearing that sweet, innocent smile. Mariel felt like screaming, but what good would that do?

Mariel stole a glance back and, sure enough, Terrell Mayfield wore a grin as big as Texas on his disgustingly handsome face—the face Mariel had been in love with since she was a freshman.

Chapter 2

"Am I seeing double or what?" Terrell asked.

Jannon giggled. "Mariel and I do look alike, don't we?" She seemed in her glory, as if she knew how much she was annoying Mariel, and she loved every minute of it.

"Mariel," Terrell called, "how come you been hiding your beautiful twin sister all these years. You got some explaining to do, girl."

"She's not my sister," Mariel said, trying to hide her fury. She knew that nothing turned a boy off quicker than a spiteful, jealous girl.

"How come you look so much alike if you're not sisters?" Terrell asked.

"I don't know," Mariel said. "I've never seen Jannon before in my life." Mariel felt like adding 'And I wish I wasn't seeing her now'. But she held her tongue. Terrell liked to flirt too much, and he was a sometimes arrogant football star. But he was the cutest, most popular boy in the class. He had been Mariel's boyfriend for a long time, making her the envy of half the other girls in school.

"Let's see now, which one of you is prettier," Terrell said. "You are both very pretty ladies, that's for sure. Let me see now, how am I going to pick between two such fair young ladies. How are they going to choose the homecoming queen when there are two of you, Mariel? Maybe this year we can have twin homecoming queens!"

Mariel's cheeks continued to burn with rage. It had been taken for granted that Mariel would be the homecoming queen. She was pretty and very popular as well as a spirited student who took part in all the activities. That this outsider might take her prize away from her made her furious almost beyond control.

"Me? Homecoming queen?" Jannon giggled. "I'd never thought of that. Oh, that would be so fun. Would I get to wear a little crown like a real queen?"

"That crown would look so fine on you," Terrell said. "Not that it wouldn't look fine on Mariel. Man, we just gotta have twin queens!" Terrell laughed at his own joke even though he knew Mariel well enough to realize how hurt she was.

All during Biology, Jannon was answering questions ahead of everybody else. So she was smart, too, like Mariel! Mariel couldn't wait for the bell to ring so she could have lunch with Lauren. She wanted to vent her anger and frustration to her friend.

"Lauren, I'm about to die!" Mariel

cried, sitting beside her friend. "My worst nightmare is happening to me. How can somebody like her just show up here?"

"I've got to admit it's weird," Lauren said.

"Lauren, how would you like a total copy of you to appear and take over your boyfriend and your life?" Mariel wailed. "It's like some evil wizard made a clone of me and sent her here to torment me!"

"Oh, don't get hysterical, Mariel. Just laugh it off, and it won't bother you so much. I mean, sure, she does look like you, but there are small differences," Lauren said.

"Mr. Webb thought she was me in Biology, *twice*!" Mariel cried. "The only thing I've got that she doesn't have is a couple of pimples!"

"Well," Lauren said slowly, "maybe … uh … she is your sister …"

"What?" Mariel almost screamed. "I

have two little sisters and one brother—
I don't have a twin sister!"

"Not that you know about ..."
Lauren said.

Mariel stared at her friend. "You
mean like Mom had twins when I was
born and one of them got sent away?"

Lauren shrugged. "I'm not saying
that happened. I'm just saying like
maybe it did. I mean, parents have se-
crets sometimes, Mariel."

Chapter 3

"That's it!" Mariel cried, her heart pounding with the terrible new knowledge she had. "Mom couldn't handle two babies at once, so she adopted Jannon out and kept me. Jannon just found out, and now she's getting even by ruining my life!"

Lauren nervously picked at her salami sandwich. "It's just a wild guess. I mean we're not sure or anything, Mariel," she said.

"But it makes sense," Mariel said. "I bet Jannon has had a miserable childhood with mean foster parents. She found out her sister had this wonderful, warm family and nice clothes and stuff. Now she wants to make me as unhappy as she is!"

"But we're not sure," Lauren insisted, sorry she had brought it up. "I could be all wrong. Don't go off all crazy and yell and scream at your Mom and accuse her of stuff that maybe didn't happen."

Mariel trembled with the awful truth. "Lauren, it all fits, the more I think about it. Mom and Dad were really young when they got married, and they were only eighteen when I was born. Imagine—eighteen year old parents with twins! Mom's really excitable anyway. Two babies at once would have been too much. Still, it was mean to send Jannon away. Now I have to pay for it. It's not fair!"

Mariel could barely sit through her afternoon classes. She was eager to get home and confirm what she suspected. She leaped on her bike after the last bell and went tearing home. She lived with her family in an apartment. Mom was a widow. Dad died shortly after the youngest child, Kara, was born.

"Mom!" Mariel cried as she charged into the apartment.

"What's wrong?" Mom called from the kitchen. "Is the place on fire or something?"

Mariel walked into the kitchen. "Mom, there's a new girl at school, Jannon Brown. She's a total dead ringer for me," Mariel said, watching her mother's face for signs of fear or guilt. But Mom's weary expression didn't change.

"Oh," Mom said, "well, stranger things have happened, I guess."

"But Mom," Mariel said, "she looks exactly like me! Like she's a twin sister or something!"

"That must make you feel strange, honey," Mom said. "Oh, do you want pizza or chicken for dinner?"

"Mom, don't you hear me?" Mariel almost screamed. "She's like a clone of me!"

"Honey, I have had a hard day at the nursing home. Nursing is tough work. I've got dinner to make, clothes to wash ..." Mom said.

"If I ever had a twin sister, it'd be her," Mariel said.

"Well, you didn't, and I'm thankful for that. Four children are enough for me. I don't think I could handle another one, especially one as full of spit and fire as you are, Mariel," Mom said.

"Is that why you gave her away?" Mariel demanded. She hadn't meant to just blurt out the accusation, but she couldn't stop herself.

Mom dried her hands and stared at Mariel for a full minute. "Girl, what did you just say? I must have misunderstood you because surely you didn't just say that I gave a baby of *mine* away, did you?"

Mariel turned numb. "But she looks like me and she even sounds like me ...

I thought maybe ..."

"You thought I gave her away? My child? Flesh of my flesh and bone of my bone? Girl, I would walk through fire and ice for my children, for you and Halle and Marcus and Kara. How can you think I'd give a twin sister of yours away?" Mom's eyes burned with anger.

Chapter 4

Mariel went to her room and tried to think. She sat on the edge of her bed, still torn by doubts. Mom did love her kids a lot. She worked two shifts sometimes at the nursing home so she could provide a nice apartment and good clothing for her children. It did seem impossible that she would have given Jannon away, but still, she was so young then. People sometimes do stupid things when they're young and scared, and then they feel guilty. And sometimes they pretend it never happened.

Mariel tried to study for her English test, but she couldn't concentrate. She kept thinking about Jannon and who she really was. She had to know!

Mariel met Lauren walking to school the next morning. "What did your mom say?" she asked Mariel.

"She got all mad when I said Jannon might be my twin sister. But I'm still not sure," Mariel said.

"Look," Lauren nudged Mariel, "there's Jannon!"

"She's with Terrell!" Mariel fumed. "Look, he's walking next to her and carrying her books! He's acting like a little puppy dog panting at her side!"

"Keep cool, Mariel," Lauren said. "Nothing turns a guy off faster than a girl being possessive. You can't act like the green-eyed monster got to you. You want to act like you couldn't care less if he hangs out with Jannon."

"Easy for you to say," Mariel snapped. "She isn't stealing your boyfriend! Oh, I'd like to just yank her hair out by the roots. I'd like to shred Terrell's football jacket, and feed it to

Jannon with chili sauce on it!"

"Chill, Mariel," Lauren said as they neared Jannon and Terrell. "Just be very cool."

Terrell was telling Jannon one of his long football stories, featuring himself as the hero. All of his stories were like that. At the crucial moment in every game, there was Terrell Mayfield to save the day. Jannon was giggling in delight, eating up every word. Mariel was sure Jannon was deliberately trying to steal Terrell from her. Everybody at school knew Mariel and Terrell were tight. Jannon had to know it, too, but she didn't care.

"Oh, hi, Mariel," Jannon said breezily. "Oh, Terrell is so funny! The way he tells a story just cracks me up. My stomach hurts from laughing."

"Yeah," Mariel said grimly, "Terrell is a funny guy all right!"

"How come you don't laugh at my stories like she does, Mariel?" Terrell asked in a teasing voice. He knew he was driving Mariel crazy by showing interest in Jannon. He was enjoying it.

"Because I've heard all your boring stories so often I can tell them myself," Mariel snapped.

"Uh-oh," Terrell grinned, his dark eyes meeting Mariel's gaze, "do I detect the hint of jealousy in your sweet voice, baby?"

"Jealous? Me?" Mariel laughed. "I'm too busy for that stuff. I'm not jealous of anybody." But Mariel's mouth was twitching, and Terrell saw right through her.

Later in the day, when Terrell was at football practice and Jannon was leaving the science building, Mariel caught up to her.

"Do you always move in on other girls' boyfriends, Jannon?" Mariel asked.

Jannon's eyes turned wide and innocent. "I thought high school was a time when we're supposed to have lots and lots of friends and not get involved with one person," she said.

"I'm on to you, Jannon. I know who you are and what you're up to," Mariel said bitterly.

"Whatever do you mean?" Jannon asked.

"Revenge," Mariel said. "That's what you want. Sweet revenge!"

Chapter 5

"Revenge?" Jannon gasped.

"Yeah. You envy me because I've had a nice life, and you got adopted out. Now you want to even the score," Mariel said.

"I don't know what you're talking about, Mariel. I have a wonderful mom and dad and a great life," Jannon said.

During her last class, Mariel racked her brain trying to think of someone in the family who would tell her the truth. Grandma and Grandpa wouldn't expose the family secret. But Aunt Leona would! Mom's younger sister was always stirring up trouble. If anybody would spill the beans it would be Aunt Leona. At every family get-together

Aunt Leona ended up causing a squabble.

After school Mariel caught a bus for Aunt Leona's apartment. If there was a discarded twin, Aunt Leona would know about it, and she'd probably tell.

"Hi, Aunt Leona," Mariel said when her aunt answered the bell. "I need to know about a skeleton in the family closet."

"Well, you came to the right place, child," Aunt Leona said, swinging open the door. "Every skeleton that ever rattled its bones in this family is known to Leona Dunn!"

"I just have to know because my whole life is being ruined by this girl who came to school looking just like me!" Mariel said. "She calls herself Jannon Brown, but I think she's my twin sister, a sister that I never was told about."

Leona had been drinking a cup of coffee and now she almost choked as she burst out laughing. "Say again?" she said.

"You mean ... it's not true?" Mariel asked in a small voice. "I don't have a twin sister that Mom and Dad gave away?"

"Child, your mama and daddy went to the hospital the night you were born in my old Rambler. You were born in the back seat! They didn't quite make it to the hospital! I can tell you, child, there was no twin sister.

"Then ... who is she? Aunt Leona, this Jannon looks just like me. She sounds like me. She just appeared out of nowhere, and she's already stolen my boyfriend," Mariel wailed.

Aunt Leona patted Mariel's hand gently. "Haven't you ever seen look-alikes, Mariel? Even famous folks have them. When I was growing up our mailman looked just like Dr. Martin Luther King, Jr. And the meter reader looked like Lyndon Johnson! Don't let this girl get to you, Mariel. Fight fire with fire. If she's sweet, you be sweeter. If she's wearing a fabulous sweater, you get one that looks even more eye-popping. Only Mariel Russell can be the best Mariel Russell in the world!"

Mariel thanked Aunt Leona and started for home. Mom was always upset when she was late, and she'd be late today. So she ran all the way to the bus stop and climbed on the crosstown bus.

"Hi," Ryan Brown said as she found a seat. "How're you doing, Mariel?"

"Oh, hi, Ryan. Okay, I guess," Mariel said. He was the quiet kid from Biology. He also played the trombone in the school band. He had a nice strong face and sparkling eyes, but he wasn't Terrell Mayfield. Terrell was the only boy on Mariel's mind.

When it was time for Mariel to get off the bus she smiled back at Ryan. "Bye, Ryan. See you."

"You bet," he said with a warm

smile.

Mariel ran from the bus to her apartment and up the stairs where the smell of frying chicken met her.

"Where have you been?" Mom demanded as she came in.

"Cheerleader practice," Mariel lied.

"Liar, liar, hair on fire," her little brother Marcus chanted. "I saw you get off the crosstown bus."

Mom came into the doorway and glared at Mariel. "I hope you never have a daughter like you are, Mariel. Maybe, I hope you do!"

Chapter 6

On Saturday Terrell and two boys were playing football on the school field. Mariel went over, anxious to put Aunt Leona's advice to work. Terrell waved at her when she arrived and came over to the fence. "Hey, baby, want to do me a big favor?" he said.

"Sure," Mariel said eagerly.

"We got a hunger for cheeseburgers, me, Luke, and Joe. Will you run down to the burger place and get us three burgers? Here's the cash," Terrell said.

Mariel didn't like the idea of a four block walk on a hot morning like this, but didn't Aunt Leona say 'If she's sweet, you be sweeter?' "Okay, Terrell," Mariel said, starting for the burger place. The hot sun burned down, and her tee shirt was wet by the return trip. But she had a white bag full of cheese-burgers. "Here you go, Terrell," she said.

Terrell and the others reached in the bag, and then Terrell slammed the palm of his hand against his temple. "Man! Where are the drinks? No cola here!"

"Yeah," Joe said. "Whoever heard of burgers and no fizz. You're a bonehead, Terrell."

"Hey, I'm looking bad to my friends, Mariel," Terrell said. "Baby, I hate to ask, but would you go for three tall, cool drinks, and get one for your-self, too."

Mariel looked at Terrell, at his big, brown eyes. She fell in love with him the night he won the championship for Grant with an incredible fumble recov-ery followed by a touchdown. They had good times together. Everybody said they made a beautiful pair—the best-looking guy and girl at Grant. That was before Jannon, of course. "Okay, Terrell, I'll get the colas," Mariel said.

"Sorry to send you off again in all this heat, baby, but me and the guys need to keep on practicing," Terrell said.

Mariel trudged down to the burger place and bought four drinks. She drank her own right away as she walked back. At the end of the trip she was really dragging. Then, as she approached the football field, she heard laughter. She paused behind the windbreak and listened to the loud voices of the boys.

"Oh, man, you think she would?" Luke asked.

"Yeah," Terrell said. "She's eating out of my hand."

"You're not sending her back for fries," Joe said. "I mean, that's cruel, man, really cruel in this heat. But it's funny, I got to admit that."

Terrell laughed again. "And when she's done bringing the fries, I'm going to send her for apple turnovers."

"Nahh, she's not that stupid," Luke said.

"Now that Jannon is sweet on me, I can get Mariel to carry my paper in her mouth and sit up and beg!" Terrell boasted. "You just watch!"

Mariel came from behind the trees, bag in hand. She pulled one of the colas out and said, "I bet you're really thirsty, Terrell, so you can have the first one." With that she hurled the tall, white paper cup at him, splashing the sticky cola on his clothes.

"Hey!" Terrell yelled.

"And since you're so nice, you can have the other two cups, too," Mariel cried, hurling both at him, one after another, thoroughly drenching Terrell in the liquid. Luke and Joe doubled over, laughing.

"I hate you, Terrell Mayfield,"

Mariel yelled. "I hate you!" She balled up the paper bag and threw that at him, too. Then she started off towards home.

Tears ran down Mariel's cheeks as she walked. Terrell was making a fool of her. He didn't care for her. Let Jannon have him. They deserved each other. But still, Mariel hurt so much she thought her heart would break.

Chapter 7

That night Marcus came into Mariel's room. "Mama told me about the girl at school who looks like you. I know who she is," he said. Mariel had been crying, but she didn't want her little brother to see that. She dried her eyes and grumbled about having to peel onions for dinner.

"What do you know?" she said.

"I know," Marcus said. "She's a bad shadow."

"A bad shadow?" Mariel asked harshly. "Is that something you read about in some stupid comic book?"

"Yeah. Comic books have good stuff in them," Marcus said. "When you're mean, like you are sometimes to Mama, then you get a bad shadow and it hangs around and makes you miserable."

"Get lost," Mariel snapped. "There's no such thing as a bad shadow, you little dummy!"

"You wish," Marcus said. "Bad shadows hang around you all the time, and sometimes they make you itch in the middle of your back where you can't scratch! And they make you forget the answers to tests, too."

"Go away," Mariel hissed. But Marcus's words hurt. If he noticed that she was mean to Mom, then there had to be truth to it. Mariel loved her mother very much, and she never wanted to hurt her. But when everything was going wrong, Mariel just got cross.

On Monday it was all over school how Mariel had turned the tables on Terrell and doused him with cola. Luke and Joe had told the story to everybody, describing in detail how Terrell was covered with sticky, sugary cola and attracting flies.

When Mariel walked into class she saw Jannon looking all fuzzy and lovely in a baby blue sweater with pearls—Mariel's favorite accessory! Mariel went over and sat beside her. "You can have Terrell Mayfield. He's all yours. You can have him with my best wishes!" Mariel said.

Jannon's eyes widened. "Oh, I don't want him. He's not my type of guy," she said.

"Oh, I get it. You just wanted to take him away from me to prove you could, but you didn't really want him," Mariel said bitterly.

"You poor thing," Jannon said. "Is that what you think? I was just nice to him, like I'm nice to everybody."

"Yeah, right," Mariel said.

At lunchtime, Mariel saw Jannon nibbling at a peach. On impulse Mariel walked over. "Your name isn't really Jannon Brown, is it?" she asked.

"Why sure it is," Jannon said.

"So where do you live?" Mariel asked.

"About two miles from here in a nice townhouse on Banyan Boulevard at 35th Street," Jannon said.

"I never saw townhouses over there. It's all empty fields," Mariel said.

"Well, we live at 7893 Banyan Boulevard," Jannon said. "Me and my parents and my two brothers. My mom teaches biology and my dad plays in the Philharmonic."

"Oh, wow," Mariel said. "You are such a good liar. I wish I knew who you really were and what you were up to!"

"I'm just a girl," Jannon said. "I'm sorry you don't like me, but maybe someday we'll be friends. I mean, miracles do happen."

"Don't hold your breath," Mariel

snapped.

Out of curiosity though, Mariel resolved to go to the corner of Banyan Boulevard and 35th Street. She would see if townhouses had sprung up in the last few months. If they had, she'd find who lived at 7893 Banyan Boulevard.

After the last period, Mariel climbed on the bus and headed east. She felt strangely excited. Maybe now, at last, she'd learn the truth about her awful twin. Maybe the mystery of Jannon Brown would be solved. After all, Jannon had ruined it for Mariel and Terrell, so the least Mariel deserved was to know why she had done it.

Chapter 8

The stores thinned out, factories appeared, and then there was nothing except open fields. When the bus reached Banyan Boulevard and 35th Street, Mariel got off. She walked to the corner and across a field filled with dried yellow mustard plants. There were no townhouses, of course, and no such address as 7893 Banyan Boulevard. The only residents who lived where that address would be were a bunch of ants on a sandy hill.

"What a liar!" Mariel muttered to herself. "I knew it." But now, more than ever, Mariel was determined to find out who Jannon was. Jannon had been at Grant only a few days and already she was making better grades than Mariel in her favorite class. And she had destroyed Mariel's relationship with Terrell.

"Hi," came a faintly familiar voice as Mariel prowled the empty field.

"Oh, hi, Ryan. What are you doing around here?" Mariel asked.

"Well, I was going to ride the bus home then I saw you get on the east bound bus, and I got worried. This is sort of a rough neighborhood and ..." Ryan said.

"You followed me?" Mariel interrupted. "Oh, that's sweet, Ryan. Uh, somebody at school said they lived here, and I was just curious," she said.

"Someday people will live here," Ryan said. "It's a fine place for a development. Maybe in fifteen years or so. But right now it's no place for a girl alone."

"When's the next bus?" Mariel asked.

"In about twenty minutes. Want to walk over to the deli and get a root beer?" Ryan said.

"That would be nice, Ryan," Mariel said, giving him a smile.

At they sipped root beer, Ryan said, "I almost asked you out a couple of times, but I always lost my nerve."

"How come?" Mariel asked.

"Terrell Mayfield."

"Oh. You thought we were really tight, huh?" Mariel said. "I guess we were. Terrell always made fun of you guys in the school marching band. Called you little tin soldiers."

"Yeah. Musicians take a lot of that, especially from the jocks. But I don't mind. Takes more than Terrell bad-mouthing me to get me down," Ryan said.

"He's such a jerk," Mariel said. "How could I have ever liked him!"

"You still sorta like him, don't you?" Ryan asked.

"Maybe," Mariel admitted. "But caring for Terrell is like having the flu. It takes time to get it out of your system, but I'm getting stronger everyday!"

"I got concert tickets for Friday. A hot little quartet—they play rock, gospel, jazz, even reggae. Want to go?" Ryan asked.

"Yeah, I'd like that," Mariel said quickly.

When Mariel got home she expected her mother would be upset that she was late again. "I just got on the east bound bus and went to see where somebody lived, Mom," Mariel explained.

"Well, at least you didn't lie about it," Mom sighed.

"Mama ..." Mariel said.

"Now what?" her mother asked.

"Mama," Mariel said, suddenly hugging her mother. "I'm sorry I'm such a pain sometimes."

"Oh, honey, it's okay. I guess it's

part of growing up. I made chicken paprika tonight. That should put everybody in a good mood. A German nurse at the home gave me the recipe," Mom said.

After dinner, Mariel was startled to see Terrell at the front door. "Baby, I'm sorry about that fool stunt I pulled with the cheeseburgers. Can we go for pizza and talk?" he asked.

Mariel shrugged. She didn't like him in the same way anymore. She never would again, but she didn't hate him either. She thought she owed him a nicer good-bye than a cola shower in the football field.

Chapter 9

Mariel climbed in Terrell's pickup, and he drove towards town. "Joe and Luke are having lots of fun at my expense," he said. "Everybody at school is laughing about how you shamed me, girl." The smile had left his face, and he looked hard and mean now. "I'm not used to being made a fool of, you hear what I'm saying?"

"I thought we were going for a pizza," Mariel said.

"You made me a laughingstock. Everybody I meet, they'll be snickering and asking me how I liked my cola bath. You're not going to get away with doing that to me, baby," Terrell said, speeding up.

"Terrell, take me home right now," Mariel yelled.

"I'll let you out," Terrell said. "But not before you learn a lesson." He sped around a corner that took them into the roughest part of town where illegal deals went down on every corner and young men leaned on storefronts looking for trouble.

Terrell screeched to a stop at a bar where half a dozen sinister-looking men stared and smirked. "Now, get out, baby," Terrell said.

"I don't have money for a taxi home," Mariel cried, dismayed.

"You are making me cry," Terrell said.

"I don't even have money to call home," Mariel said.

"Get out of my truck, baby. Maybe one of those fellas on the corner will help you out ... or maybe they'll invite you to a party ..." Terrell said.

"Terrell, unless you take me right

back home, I'm going to make so much trouble for you at school that you'll never play football again!" Mariel cried.

Terrell's eyes burned with anger and fear. Football meant everything to him. "You wouldn't dare mess up my football, baby. You wouldn't dare!"

"Take me home, Terrell, or I swear, you'll never play football for Grant again!" Mariel yelled.

The pickup leaped forward and turned around. "You think you made a fool of me, and got away with it," Terrell snarled.

"You made a fool of yourself!" Mariel shot back.

Terrell roared up to Mariel's apartment. Mariel never saw the figure standing on the sidewalk. She'd forgotten that Ryan was coming over to tell her more about Friday's concert.

Mariel grabbed the door handle and was starting to get out when Terrell gave her a violent shove, sending her sprawling onto the lawn. "That's my good-bye, girl!" Terrell yelled after her. Terrell didn't see the boy who yanked open his truck door and screamed, "Don't you ever treat her like that again, Mayfield!"

"Ryan!" Mariel cried, scrambling to her feet. "I'm okay, Ryan." Terrell was a big, chunky football player, and Ryan was a tall, lanky trombone player. But surprise was on Ryan's side. He aimed a punch into Terrell's jaw and toppled him onto the street. Then Ryan grabbed the truck keys and threw them into some bushes.

"Get out of here or I'll call the police," Mariel shouted at Terrell.

Terrell was scared, especially since some neighbors were gathering. He put up his hands and grinned sheepishly. "Okay, okay, no problem," he said, seeing his football career on the line.

When Ryan and Mariel were alone, Ryan said, "Are you over the flu for good now, Mariel?"

"And then some," Mariel sighed.

Friday afternoon at school Mariel asked Ryan who he thought Jannon really was.

"She's just a girl," he said. "A lucky girl because she looks like the prettiest student at Grant."

Mariel watched Jannon walk across the campus. "I just can't stop wondering who she is," she said.

Chapter 10

The Friday concert was great. Mariel was liking Ryan more each day. Someday maybe she might even love him. In a strange way Jannon had done her a favor by breaking her up with Terrell because that made Mariel and Ryan find each other.

Mariel looked for Jannon on Monday, but she wasn't in class. She wasn't anywhere. Mariel went to the office to find out what happened to her.

"Why, Jannon Brown has withdrawn from school," the clerk explained. "She won't be going here anymore.

Mariel felt a strange, empty feeling. She wanted to tell Jannon there were no more hard feelings. Now she wouldn't get the chance. She wanted to thank Jannon. She helped Mariel see what Terrell Mayfield and Ryan Brown were really like. Terrell was so self-centered. Ryan was so kind.

Mariel walked slowly across the campus, glancing almost forlornly at the places she used to see Jannon. The fruit machine where she got her daily peach or pear. The yogurt machine where she never failed to get the pineapple flavored kind. It didn't seem possible she was truly gone.

"Jannon is gone, Ryan," Mariel told him at lunch. "She just left school."

"Is that right? Well, she was a nice kid. We have the same last name, you know. We'd joke about that. She had a nice sense of humor."

Mariel stared at Ryan. "I didn't know you ever talked to her."

"Oh, sure. She liked music. She figured it was real nice that I played the trombone and marched in the school band. She said maybe I'd have a career in music later on. That's what I want to do, you know," Ryan said. A strange smile touched his lips then. "You know, I've got a cousin named Jannon. That's a real pretty name, and she's a favorite cousin. I thought once, if I ever have a daughter, I might want to name her Jannon."

Mariel felt the hair on the back of her neck stand up. "Ryan ... do you think we'll ever see her again ... Jannon, I mean."

Ryan took a long time to answer, then he smiled. "I think so. Yeah, I really do."

Mariel turned to Ryan and his arms came up around her, giving her a hug. For just a moment they clung to each other, half in awe and half in delight. Mariel felt safe and warm in his arms. She needed to feel that way just now because all of a sudden she knew who

Jannon Brown was. She knew why Jannon had come to Grant High School for such a brief visit. Mariel could not tell anyone what she'd learned deep in her heart because it was one of those mysteries of life that can never be explained in words.

Mariel knew that someday she would marry Ryan Brown. He would play in the Philharmonic. And they would live in a townhouse at 7893 Banyan Boulevard with their daughter, Jannon.